THE SECRET OF THE NAIL

A Faith Demeter Adventure

CATHARINE DRUM SCHERER

Life Chronicles Publishing
Give your life a voice!
Life Chronicles Publishing

ISBN- 978-1-950649-37-2

Editor: John A. Huguley

lifechroniclespublishing.com

CONTENTS

CHAPTER 1

THE DREAM

The wooden gate to the neighbor's backyard opened magically. In the dark of the night, Anna walked slowly in her light flannel nightgown. She resembled a phantom with her bare feet floating across the snow which blanketed the sleeping garden.

Anna reached the tree that seemed to call her name. Standing in front of the gnarly giant, she wondered why she was there. She knew she was looking for something — she didn't know what, until her eyes fell upon the rusty nail. It was sticking out of the tree just above her head. She could reach it if she stood on her tiptoes, but the nail was embedded deep in the bark of the tree and looked as though it had been there for a very long time.

Anna reached for the nail and took hold of it with both hands. She pulled at it, but it didn't budge. Pausing for a moment, she wondered what she should try next. She grabbed the nail again, this time giving it a slow counterclockwise turn — it moved — she turned it again, then one more time. Three twists in all. Suddenly, the tree trembled. A small imperceptible crack appeared in the bark and expanded down the trunk. Light like liquid sap began to seep through the opening. All at once there was a mighty rumbling. The tree shrugged and opened wide. Intense light streamed through the opening. A sound, indescribably clear and strong, enticed Anna closer.

Shading her eyes from the intensity of the light, she peered in.

What she saw and heard made it clear; she had to step inside.

CHAPTER 2

MORNING

It was early and the sun had not yet risen. Anna sensed the warm flannel sheets surrounding her as she slowly opened her eyes. Just waking up, she still felt like she was in a dream. Had it really happened? She needed to know. Whatever she experienced still resonated throughout her body and felt wonderful. She stretched and rolled herself out of bed. In the dark, she reached for her jeans and sweatshirt from a pile where she had placed them the night before. Without turning on any lights she dressed and made her way down the stairs through the silent house. Slipping on her coat and boots Anna opened the front door, closing it quietly behind her, and ran out into the morning air.

The sun was beginning to rise, a hint of light brightened her path. Anna made her way in the still morning to the house next door. Behind the house, there was the gate. Anna approached it slowly. This was no ordinary gate, but the entrance to a forbidden place. How had it opened so easily the night before? Anna hesitated, feeling her fear rising. For as long as she could remember, she had been told this place was dangerous. It was the backyard of The Witch, her mysterious and scary neighbor! Did she dare enter?

Anna's need to know was stronger than her fear. She unlatched the gate and moved carefully into the yard. The brown and gray colored garden was covered with an old layer of dirty snow. The tree stood in the center of a labyrinth in the middle of the garden.

Stepping over the stones that lined the labyrinth, Anna moved directly to where the nail had been in the dream. She faced the tree, scanning it up and down. All the bark was in place. There was no nail.

'It was there!' she thought, *'I know it was!'* Doubt crept in, enveloping her mind like the morning mist. Any memory she had, now evaporated. Anna returned to the gate slowly, retracing her steps.

Only a dream. She shook her head. One small remnant clung to her fading memory. The words, "You are not alone." What this meant — she hadn't a clue.

As she carefully closed the gate behind her, Anna failed to notice a pair of bespectacled eyes watching her from behind a curtained window.

Back at home, Anna removed her coat and boots. In stocking feet, she walked into the kitchen where her mother sat at the table drinking her peppermint tea and reading the morning paper. Her mother looked up briefly and smiled. Anna distractedly grabbed a bowl and filled it with oatmeal from a pot sitting on the stove. Her mother was used to her daughter's early morning ramblings, so she didn't consider this morning to be unusual. Her husband, an archeologist, would take Anna exploring in the nearby park, digging for artifacts and fossils when he was home. He would invite her to notice details, small things that might have been invisible at first. Now he was on a dig in Afghanistan, undeterred by the unrest in the region.

If her mother was frightened for him, she never let on to it. Anna, in turn, did not speak of her father.

Anna was a loner and dealt with her troubles internally. When she missed her father the most, she would hike in the woods behind her house. In all kinds of weather, she found solace just sitting on the ground in her secret spot or climbing her favorite tree, nestling in its branches reading her preferred book of the day.

"Did you sleep well?" her mother asked.

"Fine," Anna replied.

Anna was not in any mood to elaborate and wasn't sure she could explain anything about her dream anyway.

"Is your report about the composition of the earth all ready?"

Anna's research for her group's presentation on the earth's core had intrigued her enough to spend many extra hours on the Internet to find out all she could. Because she loved to read, she could sit with the encyclopedia for long stretches at a time. She had gone on to learn about the crust and the mantle, even though these were subjects her teammates would present to the class.

Anna brought her bowl to the kitchen, washed it, and put it in the sink.

In the bathroom she brushed her teeth and hair. Looking in the mirror, she sighed.

No one except her parents called Anna pretty. She thought her blue-green eyes were nice. She liked that she was strong and a good swimmer. Her short, mousy blond hair had a mind of its own when it came to brushing it. Looks or being popular was not something that worried her very much. There was no chance of either, so why bother?

Ready to leave, Anna put on her boots, grabbed her coat from the peg, and walked out the door.

She walked down her steps, turned at the sidewalk, and headed for school. She walked rapidly past the Witch's house as usual, casting only a quick glance as she sped by.

CHAPTER 3

THE WITCH

Everyone called her, "The Witch." She certainly fit the stereotype, with her wrinkled skin, gnarly limbs, wild white hair. She was rarely seen in the neighborhood, but fantastic stories circulated about her. People said her eyes could see right through you. Nobody ever wanted to be caught in her gaze. As one tale went, if you looked into her eyes you would turn into stone. Some stories about The Witch had been around so long that parents and even grandparents knew them. There was the one story about the child who had disappeared 35-years-ago without a trace. No one remembered who the child was, but The Witch certainly had something to do with it. Probably poisoned with a brew she made from the plants in her garden. Any events that could not be explained were conveniently blamed on The Witch.

Everyone said that The Witch had lived in the house all her life. The paint was now peeling off the once grand house from another era. The stone walkway to the front door was cracked and pushed up by tree roots. Dark tree limbs brushed against the mud-covered windows and made a scrutch scrutching sound when the wind blew. Only a single light appeared once in a while from an upstairs window. Now, in the bleakness of the end of winter, one could imagine the worst happening behind its walls.

On Halloween children would dare each other to run up to the front door and knock on it. No one ever did.

The Witch had a requisite black cat that sat watching from the front porch, its glowing green eyes taking in everything.

This morning the cat sat on the porch staring at Anna as she passed the house. Anna looked away and didn't see the cat's gaze following her out of sight. Nor did she see the door of the house open and the cat walking slowly inside to be picked up by wrinkled hands.

CHAPTER 4

A BAD DAY

Coming to the end of the block, Anna crossed the street at the light and turned at the corner. She then walked another short block to the school. Walking up the steps she felt confident. She was ready. She detested doing reports in front of people, but she had practiced numerous times in front of the mirror. She had worked hard on her part of the report and she knew her subject.

Anna walked into the 6th-grade classroom and fervently hoped her partners were ready. She really didn't like working in a group, but Mrs. Hale had picked her to work with Charlie and Tonya. They were to report on the earth and its layers and had a brief meeting to talk about their parts.

Charlie was a White kid. He was a quiet, shy, geek. His glasses and ruffled hair made him look the part of a mad scientist. He had been in the same class with Anna since kindergarten. She was pretty sure he would know his part. She didn't know Tonya very well, so wasn't so sure what to think about her. She was new this year, having been bussed from across town. Tonya didn't share much at all. Anna could understand being private, but Tonya seemed to have a chip on her shoulder and what Anna described as having a "fierce" expression. Anna wasn't used to having a Black classmate and hadn't really tried to get to know her. Tonya didn't seem to be friendly except with her friends. At lunch Tonya mostly hung out with the kids that came from her neighborhood.

Mrs. Hale called Anna's group up to report. Anna went first. She began, "The core makes up about one-third of the earth. The inner core is believed to be solid iron and nickel. The outer part of the core is superheated liquid iron." She went on, "Scientists say that the outer core is made of iron and is dense. They also think that movement of the outer core causes the magnetic field around the earth, moving in a counter-clockwise direction, somehow creating the North and South magnetic poles."

Charlie was next. He did a credible job with the mantle, speaking about the tectonic plates which are more pliable, can move, and cause earthquakes. These rocks can melt into magma and become lava, which breaks through the tectonic plates becoming volcanoes.

Now it was Tonya's turn. She paused for a moment before starting her part about the crust. Anna squirmed inside. '*She must need help,*' she thought, '*Maybe, she doesn't know her part.*'

Unable to contain herself, Anna quickly jumped in. "The crust is the thin outer layer of the earth, made up of mostly basalt and granite. The ocean covers seventy percent of it and the continental crust is thinner than the ocean crust. The highest point is Mount Everest. The lowest is the Mariana Trench, also known as Challenger Deep. It is so deep that if you put Mount Everest in it, there would still be a mile of water over it."

Having exhausted everything, she remembered for the moment, Anna sat down. '*The report is saved,*' she thought. '*I'm glad I could help!*'

Tonya sat silently, saying nothing. Mrs. Hale frowned.

It was time for lunch. The children in the classroom filed out to the cafeteria. Anna grabbed her lunch and was heading for the door when Mrs. Hale stopped her. "Anna, I am disappointed in you. Did you mean to cut Tonya off like that? You essentially stole her work."

Anna had no idea what Mrs. Hale meant. She was only trying to help, she thought. Anna was confused. Her face burned. She never in all her life would take someone else's work. What was she saying?

Anna was speechless. There were no words to express the entire mass of growing shame and rage that churned inside her, ready to explode. How could she be so stupid? What made her think she could make things better by covering for Tonya? Now everything was worse, and she was being blamed. She could hardly hear what Mrs. Hale said next except finally, "I expected better of you!

After a very long day in which she could barely concentrate on anything, the final bell rang. Anna loaded her books into her backpack and walked out the classroom door and down the hall, accidentally bumping into several people in her rush to leave.

To make matters worse, Tonya and her friends stood just outside the school, arms folded, glaring at her. As she passed them, Anna couldn't help but overhear the comment, "Here comes that know-it-all!"

CHAPTER 5

IN WHICH THINGS GET WORSE

Anna was so upset as she walked home, she barely noticed she was walking by The Witch's house until she felt a furry, foreign entity rubbing up against her legs. It almost tripped her. It was the black cat.

"I don't need any more bad luck, thanks." Anna fumed, feeling like kicking it out of the way. Then she thought, *'This is strange. What is the cat doing out of the yard?'* She had never seen it move from the porch.

"Go home!" Anna commanded, giving the cat a shove with her leg. The cat did not move. It seemed to lean more insistently into her leg.

"Really — go away!" Anna pushed harder. This time the creature backed up and took a flying leap, landing directly into Anna's surprised arms.

"Now what?" The problems of the day seemed pale in significance with the problem she now faced. Anna tried to shake the cat out of her arms and drop it on the other side of the rickety fence surrounding the witch's yard. The cat clung to her jacket, claws firmly attached.

There was nothing to be done but to open the front gate, make her way to the front porch, and leave the cat there. Terror soon replaced her anger and indignation. What if The Witch were to come out? What if she thought Anna was trying to steal her cat? This was an accusation that could have more dire consequences than being beaten up by Tonya's friends. Being innocent wasn't going to protect her.

Anna frantically searched up and down the street. There was no one around to notice her predicament.

If she disappeared, they might never see her again. No one would know where she went, and she would become another story like the child who disappeared 35-years-ago. She could hardly breathe as she walked as quietly as she could, legs shaking, to the porch.

She tried to release the cat one more time as she started up the stairs to the witch's front door. Her foot landed on the first step. The loose board screeched like a creature whose tail had been stepped on. The cat clung tighter. The second step was no better than the first. The third and last step was the worst of all.

To no avail, Anna tried one last time to disconnect from the black furry creature that seemed to have become a permanent growth on her chest. Then to her horror, the front door slowly swung open.

CHAPTER 6

THE MEETING

"Oh, there you are, I have been waiting for you!" The voice was soft and welcoming. Anna had heard stories of sweet voices luring people to their doom, like the Sirens lured Odysseus. She was full of dread, not knowing what was to become of her. Two arms covered in a woven gray shawl reached out.

The cat released itself from Anna's jacket and jumped into the embrace of a woman who was no taller than Anna. She wore comfortable clothes, a long skirt, and sneakers. Her face was surprisingly kind. Wrinkles adorned her eyes and lips. The age lines formed intriguing patterns on her cheeks. White hair surrounded her face like a cumulus cloud, soft and abundant. Eyes smiled from behind sparkly red-rimmed glasses.

"Please come in. I so rarely get visitors."

'No kidding,' thought Anna, still on guard. And yet this was confusing. She did seem nice. Maybe too nice. Anna felt a shiver run through her body. Should she make a run for it? There was an aura about the woman that Anna couldn't describe. The stories she had heard all her life about this dangerous and scary person collided with her experience of someone who seemed kind. Anna didn't know what to believe. The curiosity that had always made her such an eager learner, avid explorer, and had occasionally gotten her into trouble, now took over any sense of fear she was experiencing. *What might she discover in this house? Who was this person anyway?*

In the end, she removed her boots at the door and followed the shawl-draped woman into the living room.

"Oh heavens, I don't believe I have introduced myself! I am Faith Demeter, and this is Petunia," she added, gesturing toward the cat. Seeing Anna raise her eyebrows incredulously, she continued, "I know, a strange name for a black cat, but that is what she wanted to be called. And you are Anna if I am not mistaken? Please make yourself at home! I will get us some tea."

Faith disappeared into the kitchen through a curtain made of strands of wooden beads that crickled against each other softly as she passed through them.

How did she know her name? Make herself at home? *Not likely!* Anna thought. She looked around nervously. A blazing fire in the fireplace warmed her toes. The cat had stationed itself on a cushion by the fire and now followed her gaze. Finally, Anna found a large chair with big pillows, colorfully embroidered with red gold and orange patterns, and sat down.

Bookshelves containing what seemed like thousands of books covered two walls of the room.

Anna spotted several titles: *The Study of Medicinal Plants, Sunset Gardening, The Heroine's Journey, Journey into Nature, Charlotte's Web, The Secret Garden, A Wrinkle in Time.* She had read the last three.

Dried plants hung upside down from the wooden rafters that were exposed on the ceiling. The room smelled of earth and lavender.

The light was low, and the late winter afternoon sun that penetrated the west window was about to disappear. The table next to her chair bore a single lamp with a stem shaped like a tree. The lampshade rested on branches and resembled a leafy canopy. As Anna pulled the chain switch, sepia light outlined the leaves etched on the shade.

Across the room was a dusty old table where a book lay open. Curious, Anna stood up and walked over to the book and read the words at the top of the page, *Innana's Descent Into the Underworld.* Intrigued and stirred by a memory, she began to read.

Suddenly, a voice inside her cautioned, *You are in danger! Get out now before it is too late!*

Anna slammed the book shut and for a moment stood paralyzed. Then, as she moved towards the door, Faith re-entered the room.

CHAPTER 7

IN THE WITCH'S HOUSE

"Life *can* be dangerous, *and* quite puzzling!" Faith said cheerily, as she entered the living room with a tray carrying two steaming mismatched china teacups filled with a steaming liquid that smelled rather like grass or weeds or a field you might run through in the summertime. She patted the cushion of the large chair, sitting down in an adjacent one and continued, "This will cure whatever ails you!" She smiled and offered the teacup filled with the warm brew to Anna.

Anna was not sure at all she liked the sound of that. She hesitated. For the first time since she entered the house, she found her voice. "What's in this?" she asked, finally sitting down, and peering into the mug warily.

"Oh, chamomile, passionflower, and a few other things I had lying around. These were used by the Algonquin, Iroquois, and Aztecs." Faith peered over her glasses at Anna, who now had her arms wrapped protectively around her knees and was huddled way back in the chair. She clutched her teacup. Faith's eyes twinkled, "What did you think it was — poison?" She raised her teacup from the saucer and took a delicate sip of tea. "It is safe enough, and it might make you relax a bit. You've had a rough day, have you?"

Anna felt exposed! What did this woman know? How did she know? Inside her stomach was like an ocean during a huge storm, and her heart was pounding hard. Outside, she couldn't move. She gazed down at the teacup in her lap.

Faith went on. "Oh, it isn't hard to read a person, if you know what to look for. It is a matter of putting pieces together, so you get the whole picture. Then, of course, it helps if you have the correct pieces. What *can* you do, when the stories you have heard and believed come face to face with reality and they don't necessarily match?" Faith delicately took another sip of tea, peering over her spectacles at Anna.

Anna moved the teacup to her mouth tentatively. Finally, she tasted the tea. It *was* a little like drinking weeds and grass, but it sent a warmth through her, slowing her heart down and calming the waves in her stomach. What was real and what were made up stories? Was this woman going to do her harm? Was she safe? This was *so* confusing.

She decided to take a chance. Once she began sharing about her day at school, the words just tumbled out.

"The new girl in my class was having trouble with her report, so I was just helping. Now my teacher thinks I stole her work or something. Everybody is mad at me and I don't understand why."

Faith listened to every word without comment until Anna was done. It felt good to be heard and not judged.

"Is it hard for you to get to know new people?" Faith asked.

Anna shared more about what she thought about Tonya. How it didn't seem like she wanted to get to know anybody anyway other than her friends from her neighborhood. But no, she, Anna, hadn't taken the time to find out much about her either.

"Has anybody taken the time to discover who you are?"

"Well," Anna began, feeling a surprising longing to be known, "Not really. I guess my mom and dad, but not anybody else."

Finally, Faith asked, "Do you know why you are here?"

Anna shook her head. "I was just returning your cat."

Faith laughed, "So you were. And exploring my garden early this morning. No stranger has dared enter there for years. I have been waiting for you to come for a long time. Now you are here, there is much to do."

This sounded ominous! Anna jumped up. "I really should get home! My mother will be wondering where I am." Yet something kept her from running for the door.

"Are you interested in that dream?" Faith questioned.

CHAPTER 8

THE JOURNEY BEGINS

The dream! What could she know about the dream?

"I don't remember anything," Anna stated. "It was nothing."

"Then what brought you to my garden?"

"It seemed real at the time. I thought there was something in the tree. But it wasn't there. Like I said, it was just a dream."

"Dreams can be more than we know."

Did Anna sense seriousness in Faith's tone?

"Is this what you were looking for?" Faith held out her wrinkled hands. They were cupped, the right hand cradling the left. In her left hand lay the Nail.

Anna's eyes widened. She stared at the nail. What was happening? She began to remember the tree, the opening, and the beautiful sounds. She felt her heart yearning for something. The dream had been wonderful.

"There is a way to enter the tree again," Faith went on. "And apparently you have been chosen to take the journey. But you must consent with your own free will."

This was more than Anna's brain could process. *How does she know about the nail? What on earth is she saying?* Anna was afraid. But in the end, her curiosity, her strong need to know, caused her to blurt out,

"Ok, but what do I have to do?" She asked. "Will I be safe? Will it take long?"

Faith replied, "There are no guarantees. I can promise nothing. The experience can feel like a lifetime and take but a moment. You will need to trust your feelings."

Anna felt a surge of, *'what was it?'* It wasn't as if she were feeling brave. More like she just had to know what had happened in the dream. "I want to go. I am ready."

"Take the nail in your hands, bring it to your heart, and close your eyes."

Tentatively Anna took the nail from Faith and brought it to her heart. Her eyes closed. A swirling mist began to rise, surrounding her. She floated in the whiteness, feeling empty but not afraid. The mist cleared and she found herself once again facing the gnarly old tree. The way was open. The light streamed forth. Shading her eyes, she stepped in.

CHAPTER 9

IN THE TREE

The song she heard in her dream called her, beckoning with a mysterious force propelling her into the tree. As she passed the threshold, she experienced an overwhelming sensation that she was coming home.

She had stepped onto a pathway of soft green moss. Slender tree trunks stood tall at either side, their green canopy forming a high archway, a grand entrance to…what? There, in the distance, she saw what seemed to be the source of the light. As she moved towards it, the song grew in complexity. Woven in were the sounds of flowing water and a soft breeze.

Following the path, Anna finally stepped into a garden where flowers of every hue bloomed in great abundance. A green willow bowed over a fountain that sent cascades of water into streams that flowed throughout the garden. It seemed that the fountain, the streams, and the flowers were joining together in the song.

Listening closer, she heard the sound of voices singing. It was the most beautiful song she had ever heard. Too exquisite to put into words, it seemed to vibrate throughout every cell in Anna's body — attuning each of her senses to a heightened awareness.

The melody of the song was profoundly familiar like an old friend found again after a long absence. Anna sang in recognition and from her mouth a sweet and clear sound blended with the company of invisible singers.

As she sang, she moved eagerly to the center of the garden. Her eyes, ears, and heart, in truth, her whole being, were full of the beauty of the place. She looked around to find the other singers.

They began to appear all around; graceful creatures who appeared human, both ancient and young at the same time. Some had skin as black as night, some as pale as a white rose. There were those with every hue in between. They wore long and flowing clothes. Some wore bright and striking colors, and some wore colors that were more muted. The beings who wore bright clothes were singing the bright melody parts of the song and the ones wearing softer colors sang a lilting, flowing harmony.

They were dancing in and among the flowers and around the fountain, circling the willow which was swaying to the rhythm of the song. Anna rubbed her eyes, looking at the willow again. The branches seemed to become dark arms clothed in flowing green, which cascaded down what had now become the body of a woman, tall and graceful, with long hair that moved in the audible breeze.

As she drew closer, Anna could see the woman's eyes. They seemed to mirror the blue of great distant mountains, the depths of the ocean, and the vast expanse of the sky. She dropped her own eyes to the ground, trembling with a feeling of awe.

Anna had never seen anyone so beautiful. It was not just physical beauty. There was a loving energy that seemed to emanate from her. Her words of welcome rang through the song, and Anna heard them, not with her ears alone, but with every cell in her body.

"How glad I am to see you Beloved One! I have called you here out of time to remind you that you are loved and that you are never alone."

Anna's head slowly rose until her eyes met the eyes of this being, the Tree Woman. Serenity and wonder filled her.

The Tree Woman spoke, "I am the Mother of every mother who has ever lived. I watch over you when you are sad or lonely, and when the pain of your world seems more than you can bear. I am there even when you cannot feel my presence. I have loved you forever and ever."

Anna felt strong warm arms wrap around her, and a loving kiss placed on her forehead. She wished she could stay always, feeling so loved.

"Is this a dream?" she asked, "It feels so real."

"The two are not exclusive," responded the Tree Woman. "In this place, you can find guidance and solace. You will also wrestle with demons." A vague uneasiness churned in Anna's stomach, as the fear of a pending nightmare began to creep in.

The Tree Woman responded gently, "In fact, you have demons that await your coming. But that is not for now, and you will not meet them without help, or until you are ready.

Anna's fear subsided when again, she felt the arms of the Tree Woman wrap around her and heard her repeat quietly, "You are never alone. There are guides and helpers in this place and in the life you live every day. You will not see me again in this form, but I am with you always."

"But where am I going? What am I supposed to do?" Anna felt the arms that had embraced her gently drift away, leaving her with the question. The mist arose again and surrounded her.

Gradually Anna found herself sitting in the large chair surrounded by big pillows. She smelled lavender and the wood smoke of the fire. She opened her eyes and they slowly began to focus. They came to rest on the nail lying in her hand. She slowly looked up and found Faith sitting across from her, holding knitting needles with the beginnings of what seemed to be a blanket cascading down her lap. Faith looked at Anna with a gentle curiously.

"I remembered," Anna whispered as if speaking out loud would break the spell. "It was wonderful!"

"You met her," Faith said simply.

"She is so beautiful! I wanted to stay forever. Can I go back?"

"When you do, it will not be the same. Cherish this moment." Faith went on, "What did she say to you?"

"That I am never alone, and dreams are real, and I have guides. Oh, I felt so much love." Anna went on, searching for the words to describe the song, the colorful creatures, the fountain…

Faith listened with a smile. Then her expression changed as she asked, "What else did she tell you?"

“Something about demons,” Anna said hurriedly, "but I don't see how there can be demons in a place like that."

“Demons will meet you wherever and whenever it is time…they most assuredly are inescapable…”

“What do you know about demons?” asked Anna, doubt and fear creeping back into her mind. *This was The Witch she was talking to after all. Had she been lured in so deeply?*

“Oh, I have wrestled with a few of my own demons. I suspect that is why I am to be your guide.” Faith seemed to drift off somewhere, recalling a hidden memory. Abruptly she returned, “For now, you must get home. I am sure your mother is wondering where you are. You will have to trust your heart on this one, my dear. You have embarked on a journey. There is no going back. You have been told that you have guides. Everyone has them, of course, but not everyone gets to know and experience them.

The nail will assist your comings and goings. For now, I recommend you allow me to keep the nail and to be with you when you go into the dream world. It makes it easier to come back."

Anna worried, "Could I get caught in a dream?" She gingerly placed the nail into Faith's outstretched hands.

"Sometimes it helps to have someone who knows how to find you," Faith replied, tucking the nail into the deep pockets of her skirt. "Now get along home. Your mother is waiting."

CHAPTER 10

THE SUMERIAN CONNECTION

When Anna walked out the door into the twilight, the squeaking steps were no longer frightening. Anna carried the warm glow of the dream with her as she walked home. Her mother had dinner waiting and she did not seem surprised at Anna's tardiness. A warm hearty soup with homemade bread was comforting. They didn't speak as they ate. Anna did not share the difficulties at school. Her mother didn't ask. Nor did Anna share the meeting with Faith, the wonder of the journey inside the tree, or meeting the Tree Woman. It was all more than her words could describe.

Her mother did not pry. They did the dishes together and tidied the kitchen.

That night after finishing her homework, she got onto the computer. There was an email from her dad! He had been out of communication for weeks, so she eagerly opened the letter.

"Dear Earthworm,"

(He had given her this name when she was little, rolling in the mud with abandon. She certainly had outgrown it, and, while normally annoyed by its use, she felt oddly comforted at the moment.)

"As you know I cannot disclose my whereabouts as we were brought in undercover to do research on the tablets containing the myth of Innana. Remember I told you the story? Well, the last tablet was never found. Some say that tablet was destroyed. But no one is sure. I think this email is secure enough to tell you that we may be close to the spot where it may be found."

Anna startled! Innana! She remembered now what had been stirred standing in the front of the open book in Faith's house. When she was younger before her father became so busy, he would tell her the story of Innana and her descent into the underworld as a bedtime story. Her mom had complained that it was too gory, but Anna always wanted to hear it anyway.

According to the ancient Sumerian myth, Innana was the Queen of Heaven, the goddess of light, love, and life. She was more beautiful than you could ever imagine.

Her sister, Ereshkigal, ruled the Underworld. She was as cruel and heartless as Innana was loving and kind.

Nevertheless, Innana felt compelled to visit the underworld, perhaps to free her beloved, some say. She adorned herself in all her radiance and finery, jewels, and rich clothing. On her head, she wore a crown.

She came to the first gate. The keeper of the gate, servant of Ereshkigal, had been instructed that Innana should get no special treatment. Like all who entered the Underworld, she was to be stripped of her earthly possessions. This was, after all, the Land of No Return.

At the first gate, she relinquished her crown.

At the second her necklace was taken.

At the third, her golden ring was taken.

At the fourth, her Jeweled shoes were removed.

At the fifth, her garments were removed.

At the sixth, her radiant spirit was taken.

At the seventh, she was bowed low.

Bowed low, in deepest despair before the throne of Ereshkigal, she was pierced by the eyes of death, and her corpse was hung from a stake to rot.

There was more to the story… Anna would recall it again when there was time. She read the last line of her father's email, "You will not be able to contact me. I will try to email you when I can. It is dangerous to communicate from where we are but don't worry, I'll be careful."

She longed to have her father safe. To hear his stories again. To share what was happening to her!

Anna turned off the computer, got up, and went into the bathroom to get ready for bed. She washed her face and brushed her teeth. She came out and found her old nightshirt, which was one of her dad's old extra-large t-shirts, lying on the floor by the bed, put it on, and crawled under the covers.

Normally she would be reading a good book, but her mind was full of the experiences of the day. The difficulties at school, the surprise meeting with The Witch, and the magic of the dream. She stayed awake for a while reflecting until her eyes grew heavy and she drifted off.

CHAPTER 11

INTO THE DARKNESS

She was trapped! Ensnared by what, she couldn't see in the total blackness. She felt her arms, legs, and chest wrapped by something strong… What were they? Arms? Hard ropes? Something was restraining her. It was hard to breathe. There was heaviness and a smell of moist earth coming into her nostrils. Where was she? Anna struggled to free herself, her muscles tensing. She felt a growing fear rising inside.

"I am strong," she thought, "I can escape." The harder she tried, the tighter she was caught. The fear made it worse as she fought this invisible adversary. She was running out of air. Why couldn't she figure this out?

"This is a dream," she reminded herself, "I am really asleep in my own bed." Then why did it feel so real, as real as the first dream, and as terrifying as it was wonderful? She wasn't waking up. The damp earthy smell seemed to weigh down on her as the hard restraints continued to hold her.

Why could she hear Faith's words coming to her now? *"Life can be dangerous and puzzling!"* What did she need to do? She searched for answers, for a way out.

Puzzling… puzzles… Anna let her mind wander. Games… tricks… what was that thing that her dad had bought her at the fair a few years back? That tube that grabbed your index fingers when you inserted them into either end and tried to pull them out. The more you pulled, the harder it held on. It was only when you relaxed that you were able to release your fingers. Could that work here?

She allowed the muscles in her arms and legs to relax. Her chest released, and her lungs began to breathe more freely. She began to feel movement in her fingers and toes as she gently wiggled them.

"Do you require assistance?" came a voice close to her head. She felt whiskers tickle her earlobe. Anna relaxed more, enough to turn her head to come face-to-face with the snout and beady little eyes of a mole. "It is clear to me that you lack the equipment to dig. And how you got here is beyond me!" the mole humphed. He began tunneling around Anna's body, loosening the soil. Finally, she was free to move. The mole began tunneling upward, "Follow me," he motioned with his sharp digger claws.

As Anna moved to free herself, she saw the large ancient roots that had held her captive. She looked in the distance and saw another life form. It was human and was also trapped. Suddenly she realized who it was — Tonya! What was she doing in her dream? The mole paused, "We can help that one too."

CHAPTER 12

IT GETS NO LIGHTER

Anna's mom woke her early for swim practice. The late winter dark still surrounded her as she put on her racing suit and stuffed her towel, goggles, and cap in her sports bag. She was surly and disagreeable. Her muscles were feeling tense as if her body really had been stuck in the roots of a tree.

Anna kept repeating to herself, *'It was a dream — but why does it feel so real?'*

She remembered the Tree Woman's words, "*The two are not exclusive…*" and "*…you can find guidance and solace. You will also wrestle with demons…*"

I don't want to deal with this right now, Anna thought as she arrived at the pool. No more thinking about demons and dreams. The workout was hard. She felt like she was swimming through mud. She was so agitated she barely noticed what was going on around her.

"Hey, watch it!" A teammate grabbed her foot as she made a flip turn, almost kicking him in the face. "We're on 50's now, we finished the 100's. What is with you?"

Anna glared and didn't respond. The workout ended. She showered and dressed. Riding home in the car, she said nothing. Her mom did not press for conversation.

Anna quickly ate breakfast and headed out the door for school. While passing Faith's house, she looked toward the porch. There was no sign of the cat. As she reached the edge of the yard, she noticed a folded piece of paper taped to the corner of the fence. It had her name written on the outside. She unfolded the note and read it. "Please join me for tea after school. Faith." That was all. Anna wasn't sure if it was an invitation or a command. She stuffed the note in her pocket.

Anna walked the next few blocks to school, hardly noticing anything. It was only when she walked up the steps into the school that she remembered the unpleasantness of the previous day. Once the memory came back, the rest of the day was filled with it. As she sat through class, Anna became angrier and angrier, as she recalled how wrongly she had been treated. When lunchtime came, she realized that she had left her lunch at home on the counter. Great! Now she was going to be hungry too. There was something deliciously satisfying about having yet one more thing to complain about. She filled herself with her misery as she sat by herself in the lunchroom. Her surroundings helped. It was a lunchroom filled with the typical debris. No matter how hard the janitors cleaned, by the end of the first lunch the floors were sticky and littered with wrappers and food. The tables were spotted with crumbs and spilled liquids of various colors.

Tonya entered the cafeteria with her friends, glanced angrily at Anna, and went to sit at the other end of the room, passing tables of boys eager to taunt and tease. One of the boys made a mean remark. He said that their hair was ugly and frizzy, poking at their heads with his finger.

Anna looked on, torn. On the one hand, Tonya deserved to feel bad, she thought. On the other hand, Anna herself had been the brunt of jokes by those same boys, called ugly, nerdy, and worse. Nobody should have to endure that abuse. Anna squirmed uncomfortably. She turned away, toward the window. A flash of orange and grey called her eyes to attention.

There, landing on the bare branch of a tree, was a robin, staring intently into her eyes, or so Anna imagined. *'You are early,'* Anna thought, *'Spring isn't coming for another month.'*

The bird, unconcerned about this fact, began to sing; one ascending long note, two lower short ones, then another long ascending note, repeated again and again.

His small orange breast offered a delicate contrast to the massive, sludgy disarray, which seemed to surround Anna inside and out.

That afternoon was a blur. By the time school was out she was eager to leave into the cold air and sunshine on her way to Faith's. The robin (the same one from lunch) greeted Anna. It led her, flying from tree to tree, stopping on the fence post outside the old house, breaking into nonstop song.

Petunia curiously came down from the porch, eyeing the robin with a cat's discerning interest. Then she turned to focus on Anna. Once again, she jumped into her arms as Anna opened the gate and entered the yard. This time it felt like comfort, and she cradled the cat. The stairs made the same sounds as before, but today she noticed they didn't evoke the same terror as yesterday.

Before she could knock the door opened, and Faith greeted her with open arms. At that moment Anna realized how long it had been since she had been hugged. Her last physical contact had been running into someone in PE, and before that, in the pool when her leg was grabbed. She rarely let her mom hug her anymore.

It felt nice to be wrapped up in the arms of Faith, who smelled of lavender and other unidentifiable earthy smells. Together they walked into the living room.

“Have a seat.” Faith said. “Would you like some tea?”

Anna nodded and sat in the old chair. Faith poured a brew from her teapot into two different unmatched china cups. The tea had chamomile in it, that she could tell. Remembering yesterday and thinking, '*was it only yesterday?*' There was something else in the tea with a little bite to it.

"Let us begin," Faith commanded, "Tell me about your dream last night."

Anna began to recall as best she could, how she had been trapped in the roots and had relaxed to free herself, about the mole, and that was it.

"There is something missing here," Faith commented. "What else?"

Why did she always know? Anna didn't relish sharing the part where she had left Tonya. Sure, she deserved it, but as Anna shared that part, she began to feel horrible.

Strangely, Faith did not seem to judge her. "We are all doing the best we can at any given moment. And we always have a chance to make other choices."

"Anyway, it was just a dream," Anna said, relieved.

In what felt like a dramatic shift, Faith responded with a firm clear voice, "Our dreams wake us to what is real. Tell me about how Tonya was in school today!"

Anna recalled images of the lunchroom. Conflicting feelings swirled inside. Being mean was not her nature, but the resentment she carried from the day before took over. What difference did it make anyway? Why did Tonya matter? She was not a friend. In fact, they certainly didn't like each other. The question made her feel surly and disagreeable again.

"We encounter others to learn more about ourselves. You must release yourself to release others," Faith said emphatically. What did that mean? Anna couldn't fathom it.

Then with more kindness, Faith spoke. "It is time to take the next step in the journey. You will not be going anywhere I have not been, although it will be different for you. You will go alone but will find companions along the way. When you feel most lost, you will be found." Faith took the old nail from her pocket and held it out to Anna.

Anna put her hands behind her back. "Hey, I don't even understand what you are asking me to do," Anna's voice grew louder and faster. She was filled with concern. "What does Tonya have to do with me and what does any of this have to do with anything?"

"You must take the next step in the journey before that question will be answered."

"I'm not going! You can't make me! This is all just stupid anyway!" Anna's fear overtook her, and she blurted out, "I'm not going to let a witch have power over me!"

The moment the words were out of her mouth she regretted them, but she couldn't shake the feeling of fear. Faith did not seem surprised at the outburst. She sat quietly and patiently until Anna was finished yelling.

"You would not have a witch have power over you, and yet you are controlled by something that will not let you go easily," Faith said quietly.

"I don't know what you are talking about."

"Are you willing to find out?"

"Do I have a choice?"

"I cannot answer that."

"So, I don't have a choice?"

"There is always a choice. As you have already chosen to come this far, the choice is to take the next step, now or later. Fighting the inevitable is a little like pulling harder on the finger trap. The harder you struggle, the more difficult things become."

Astounded, and once again wondering how Faith could connect with her dream, Anna worked at calming herself and listening. But she had to ask, "Am I going to meet a demon? Tell me what to do!"

"I can offer you two things; First, a riddle. "What is higher than the sky, deeper than the Mariana Trench, is all around you and deep inside? The answer will help you with any demon you might encounter."

Anna pondered what she knew. What is all around us and deep inside? Water? Air? Nature? Knowledge?

Faith continued, "Second, do not hesitate to use the help offered to you by your guides. This will be harder for you than you can imagine."

Before Anna could consider this, she felt The Nail pressed against her palm. As she became aware of its presence, she found herself once again in the mist on her way to another place.

CHAPTER 13

A FAMILIAR PLACE

When the mist cleared, she found herself in a meadow. It was warm and inviting. Flowers, purple, gold and white, bloomed in abundance. Anna began to relax. She sensed she had been here before, but when and where? When a head with beady eyes and a long snout popped out of a hole, she knew. It was the place she last saw the mole after he had tunneled them out from underground.

"So, you're back," he humphed again in his particular manner. "Unfinished business no doubt. Can't go leaving humans trapped underground, now can we? Shall we be off?"

"Off to where?" Anna inquired, "I really haven't been told what I am to do here?"

"No? Well, my goodness, isn't it OBVIOUS?" the mole asked incredulously.

"I am afraid not," Anna replied.

"You left a friend in a rather difficult position. I assumed you came back to make it right."

Anna was feeling angry. Tonya hadn't done her part on the report. Anna had just tried to help which got her in trouble with the teacher and might get her beaten up. Why was she being asked to make it right?

"She isn't my friend and it really isn't my problem. She probably got *herself* stuck there. And anyway, I figured a way to get out all by myself, why can't she?"

The mole couldn't contain himself, "What do they teach where you come from? How would you know a friend? — Do you know the struggles Tonya has?

She has her own demons. She wasn't trying to mess up the report. And she didn't need your help, at least not the way you offered it. Do you have any idea how embarrassed she felt?"

The mole paused to let Anna consider this last question. Then he continued emphatically. "How we do limit ourselves and others when we assume the worst. — And, by the way, you did not get out of your last predicament by yourself. You did have help!"

Anna could hardly hear what the mole had said. How did he know so much about Tonya? *And what about me?* She felt so enraged and misunderstood. She was about to retort in her own defense, when out of the corner of her eyes she detected a slight movement in the grass, as if there was a small wind at ground level, pushing the grass forward — towards her.

She followed the motion curiously. All at once, a giant head rose right in front of her. Huge, sharp devouring teeth inside a pus-filled open mouth filled her vision. Anna screamed, unable to move.

CHAPTER 14

THE DEMON

The demon was horrifying. So horrifying it distracted her from something worse. Afraid she was going to be eaten, she did not notice that pus from its mouth was dripping down to her feet. Whatever was in this oozing mess began to cause first her feet to become numb. Gradually it rendered each part of her body that it touched to have no feeling. After her feet came her legs, then her knees, thighs, and hips. As it moved up her torso, she found she could not breathe. It covered her face and continued to seep through her ears into her brain. At first, afraid and angry, Anna fought this invasion. The more she fought, the more strongly the pus flowed from the mouth of the hideous creature. With one last huge effort, Anna tried to escape, to rid herself of this force that was taking over her entire being.

Instead, Anna swirled deep down into darkness. It was as if she was nothing in the middle of nothing. She could not feel her body, nor could she hear, see, or smell.

The thread that held the question, "What is higher than the sky and deeper than the Mariana Trench?" in her mind was unraveling. What could help her now? What was all around and deep inside her? There was nothing.

Something was sucking everything out of her. There was an entity of massive proportions that she could not see or hear or touch — a grey mass with no defined shape, sending out oozing tentacles into the crevasses of her mind and through every pore of her body. Where each tentacle touched, a great fear and misery overtook her. The thread had broken, and Anna fell into the deepest despair.

By the fire, Faith sat quietly. Listening. Waiting for the moment. Now. Her hand reached out. The index finger of her left hand alone pointed toward the heart of the slumped and empty form that was Anna.

CHAPTER 15

FOUND

Into the pit of empty despair came a small almost imperceptible sensation. A sense that SOMETHING or SOMEONE was looking for her, seeking her out. From the one place the grey tentacles could not penetrate came a stirring. The stirring caused a vibration to spiral out from the center of her heart, down her spine, and throughout her body. The vibration became a sound, the sound became a song with no words. Then slowly, slowly, Anna began to feel and sense the question, *'What is higher than the sky and deeper than the Mariana Trench?'* Whatever IT was, was trying to find her.

The vibrations grew stronger, loosening the hold of the tentacles. The song surrounded her, filled her. She found her voice and sang a response. She felt her body tingle like it had been asleep and was now waking up.

In the song she heard her words, "I am there even when you cannot feel my presence. I have loved you forever and ever."

Love! Higher than the sky, deeper than the Mariana Trench. Love was finding her even in the darkest place, filling her, wrapping her up in warm arms.

She smelled the warm, familiar, earthy smell of lavender and Faith. She felt arms holding her. The familiar song now sung simply by one voice was in her ears. Opening her eyes slowly, she took in the vivid colors of the yarn in the knit blanket that wrapped around her, feeling its softness against her skin. The warm flames in the fireplace danced before her.

Petunia lay cuddled close to her, both of them sharing Faith's ample lap.

There were no words spoken right away. Faith offered a piece of warm muffin, placing it gently in Anna's mouth. It tasted like nothing she had ever tasted before, with a sweet delicious flavor melting on her tongue.

Every sensation felt new and rich. Anna took in each sight, taste, smell, sound, and touch, allowing each experience to fill and nourish her.

She was forgetting something…

"Oh, I left Tonya trapped! I need to find a way to help her!"

"You have already begun. You have taken quite a journey," Faith answered quietly.

"But I didn't do anything."

"Sometimes the only thing to do is to be with what is right in front of you. Doing your own work. That is all. Then see how things transform around you. Ask the question, 'What Would Love Do?'"

"That's it?"

"Yes"

It was time to leave. Anna embraced Faith with a strong hug. Faith placed a book in her arms.

"Be tender with yourself," Faith offered, "See what has changed. Come be with me anytime. I love you."

Anna put on her jacket, opened the door, and stepped into the cool early night air. It smelled of the moist earthy spring to come, the sun offering its last rays to light her way home. She reached the gate and turned one last time to see Faith and Petunia standing still in the doorway, silhouetted by the firelight behind them. From out of the gentle darkness came the sound of the robin, one ascending long note, two lower short ones, then another long ascending note, repeated again and again.

As she opened the gate and closed it behind her, she knew she would be back again before long. Her mother was waiting at the door, greeting her with a hug and a kiss on the head. Anna did not turn away, receiving it gratefully.

"I have missed you, Anna. I am so glad you are home."

In bed that night, Anna read,

"Innana lay dead three days and three nights. On the fourth day, when she had not returned, Ninshubur, her loyal friend goes to the Gods for help. Only Enki, God of water and creativity agrees to help and devises a plan to restore Innana to life.

From the dirt under his fingernails, he creates tiny creatures called kurgarru, and gives to them the "food and water of life." Tiny and insignificant, they slip unnoticed into the underworld where they meet

Ereshkigal wailing and grieving the death of her husband.

These little creatures minister to her and tend to her in her need. In her gratitude, she grants them one wish. They ask to revive Innana. This request she grants. And the kurgarru sprinkle the food and water of life on Inanna's corpse.

Innana revives and goes forth from the underworld, back to the world of the living."

CHAPTER 16

NEW BEGINNINGS

Anna awakened from a peaceful sleep. She felt empty yet full at the same time. *What will this day bring?* Walking out the door, she heard a familiar sound. The robin greeted her with its song and followed her. At Faith's gate, Anna paused. The formerly bare yard was now blooming yellow, red, purple, and green. Violets, tulips, daffodils, and other flowers Anna could not name, signaling the coming of Spring. Changes. The robin waited and accompanied her to school.

Entering the classroom, Anna ventured a glance in Tonya's direction. Tonya kept her head down, working on some classwork, and did not look at Anna at all.

Class began. Then, when the bell rang for recess, Mrs. Hale called Anna and Tonya to her desk, "The two of you have some work to do. I would like you to spend some time this afternoon after school together, just the two of you." This sounded more like an order than an invitation.

Tonya had a bus to catch, she said. Mrs. Hale replied that she would drive Tonya home herself even after Tonya let her know how far away she lived. Anna could think of no excuse. There was no getting out of it.

That afternoon after the last bell rang, they sat side by side, facing the front of the class. A long awkward silence ensued.

With some hesitation Anna broke the silence, "I am sorry. I think I made some assumptions the other day and I guess I am wondering if you would let me fix whatever I did wrong."

With mixed emotions, Tonya replied, "I don't know why I have to point it out. It seems pretty obvious. You basically took over the report before I had a chance to say a word."

"I was just trying to help. I didn't know you were ready." Anna struggled to control her defensiveness.

"Well, I was. I don't know what makes you think you were helping anyway. What makes you think I wasn't ready, and I needed your help?"

This question caused Anna to pause and consider it. What had made her jump in so quickly? It was disconcerting to discover that a part of her had felt somehow superior cloaked in the guise of being helpful.

Tonya continued, "We are both in the same advanced class. I could have said everything you did and more. Did you know the Tibetan name for Mt. Everest is Qomolangma or Holy Mother?"

"Holy Mother?" Anna's eyes widened. "I am sorry" repeated Anna.

"You embarrassed me in front of the whole class. Now they probably really think I am stupid or lazy or something."

At that moment Mrs. Hale entered the room. She looked at Tonya, "I am glad you have had a chance to share and that Anna has apologized. What more can Anna do to make amends?"

Tonya took a deep breath. She found she had no more to say.

Mrs. Hale turned to Anna, "You have apologized to Tonya. What if you apologize in front of the class?"

Tonya's face brightened and a smile began to show on her face. Anna was flabbergasted. *'Why am I being asked to embarrass myself? I did apologize! This is too much!'*

She felt that familiar upset and defensiveness begin to rise yet again, and she said nothing.

Mrs. Hale continued, "I know this may be hard for you Anna, but I am asking you to sleep on it and consider it. I will check in with you in the morning."

Without a word, Anna grabbed her backpack and headed out the door. As she walked down the steps, she heard a familiar few notes. There on a lower branch of the tree just outside the school, she saw the robin. It seemed as if his song was definitely for her. It was an insistent joyful tune. Her defensive barriers began to melt.

The robin accompanied her to the gate of Faith's house. There Anna found a new note. She gently unfolded it. "What Would Love Do?" is all it said.

No longer surprised that Faith seemed to know what was happening in her life, Anna pondered the question, "*What would love do?*" She knew the answer. *But does it have to be so hard?*

That night she slept deeply. She didn't remember her dreams. Yet when she awoke, she felt strong and held. As if love had visited her in the night and given her the courage to do what she knew she must. An early morning melody sang outside her window, reinforcing her resolve.

As she walked to school, she came once again to the now welcoming home of Faith who was standing on her front porch, Petunia in her arms. She smiled deeply, waved, and blew a kiss to Anna, who paused to take in the love.

When she arrived at school, Anna entered the classroom and nodded at Mrs. Hale. who brought the classroom to attention. "Anna has something to share."

Looking at Tonya, Anna began, "I made a mistake the other day. I thought Tonya wasn't ready and I took over her part of the report. I embarrassed her. She *was* ready and knew more than I did. I am sorry you didn't get to hear what she had to say. She taught me to not be so quick with my assumptions and that the Tibetan name for Mt. Everest is Qomolangma or Holy Mother, among other things."

Once Anna got started, she found it wasn't as hard as she expected. It was as if a huge load was lifted from her shoulders. She looked at Tonya and acknowledged, "I know I have a lot more to learn. Thank you!"

ACKNOWLEDGMENTS

It has taken 65 years of my life and many helper spirits along the way to bring this story to life.

I am grateful to the unseen spirit who sent me the original dream when I was 4 years old. It was as real then as it is in this book.

As an adult, when the story began to unfold and I was still looking for the Nail, I met Madeleine L'Engle (author of *A Wrinkle in Time*) at a conference. When I shared the story, she encouraged me to keep looking, saying she was sure I would indeed find the Nail.

Years later when I visited Hawaii, Barbara Robinson, an author and English teacher and mother of my best friend in 6th grade, invited me to get the story ready for a children's short story contest. It won honorable mention and $25!

Years later I read the story to Molly Zammit's 3rd and 4th grade class at Discovery School in Spokane, WA. Alec, Andrew, Dylan, Jadwin, Kira, Michael, Pierce and Samantha told me then it should be a chapter book.

More years later Molly's class, Patty, Rachel, Aislyn, Imani, Maya, James, Sam, Mirabai, Zack, Sarah, Dan, Lavinia, Chloe, Aden and Gwyn heard the first version of the chapter book. They offered me their questions, and creative ideas. They also shared their stories and pictures with me. Being together with them was a wonderful and important part in the unfolding of the story.

Along the way, I had initial publishing and editing support from Charlotte Pierce of Pierce Press, Susan, and Chris Noel. Then back into a file drawer it went for another few years.

When it was revealed to me that the important conflict in the book was to be between a white girl and a black girl, I realized I had much to learn, and called on Dr. Roberta Wilburn, diversity trainer and professor at Whitworth University in Spokane, to provide her deep wisdom and to give voice to Tonya.

As the book became what you read today, friends and family offered their help as readers, editors, and midwives. Thank you to Marsha Moyer, Greta Sorenson, Cyd Dudgeon, Bridget Culligan, Dia Walker, Sarah Brody, Bonita Zahara, Judi Julien,

JoBeth Eckerman, KT Norton and especially Ruth Kittleson and Molly Zammit.

Finally, in the careful hands of Sharon Blake and her team at Life Chronicles Publishing, the book has taken final form. Their editing and finishing touches have brought this story home!

Molly Zammit thank you for pushing and prodding me through this process, always asking, "What about the book?" even when it waited, hidden in a dark file.

As it turns out, this is just the beginning of the journey. Who knew?

May we each continue to share our own stories with those who will listen and receive them

Made in the USA
Columbia, SC
07 January 2025

49134731R00062